Daddy Hugs

For
Tom
and
Cristina

N A N C Y T A F U R I

Daddy Hugs

L B

Little, Brown and Company

New York   Boston

Little ones love hugs.

"I love drippy hugs," says Little Turtle.
"Just-Daddy-and-me hugs."

"I love soggy hugs,"
says Little Beaver.
"Just-Daddy-and-me hugs."

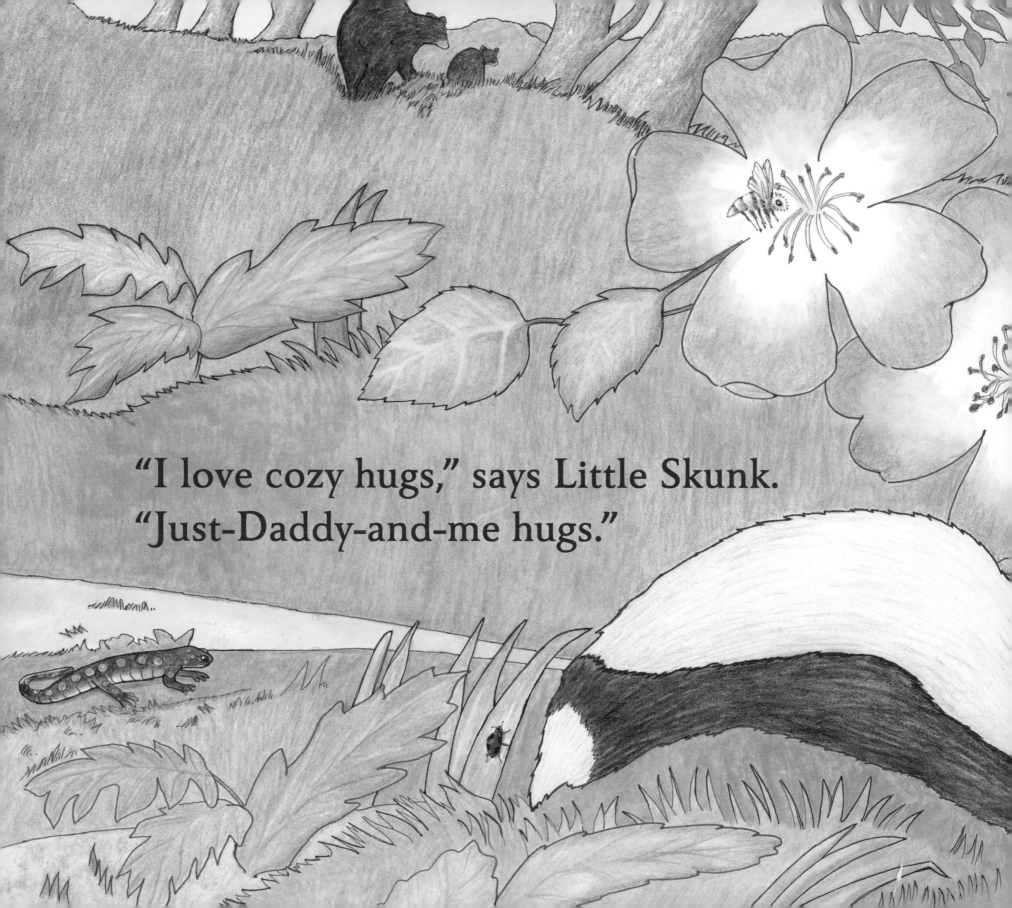

"I love cozy hugs," says Little Skunk.
"Just-Daddy-and-me hugs."

Eeepy-eeep-eeep!

Rurrr-rurrr-rurrr!

"I love furry hugs," says Little Bear.
"Just-Daddy-and-me hugs."

"I love whiskered hugs," says Little Fox.
"Just-Daddy-and-me hugs."

Chip-chip-chip!

"I love fuzzy hugs," says Little Chipmunk. "Just-Daddy-and-me hugs."

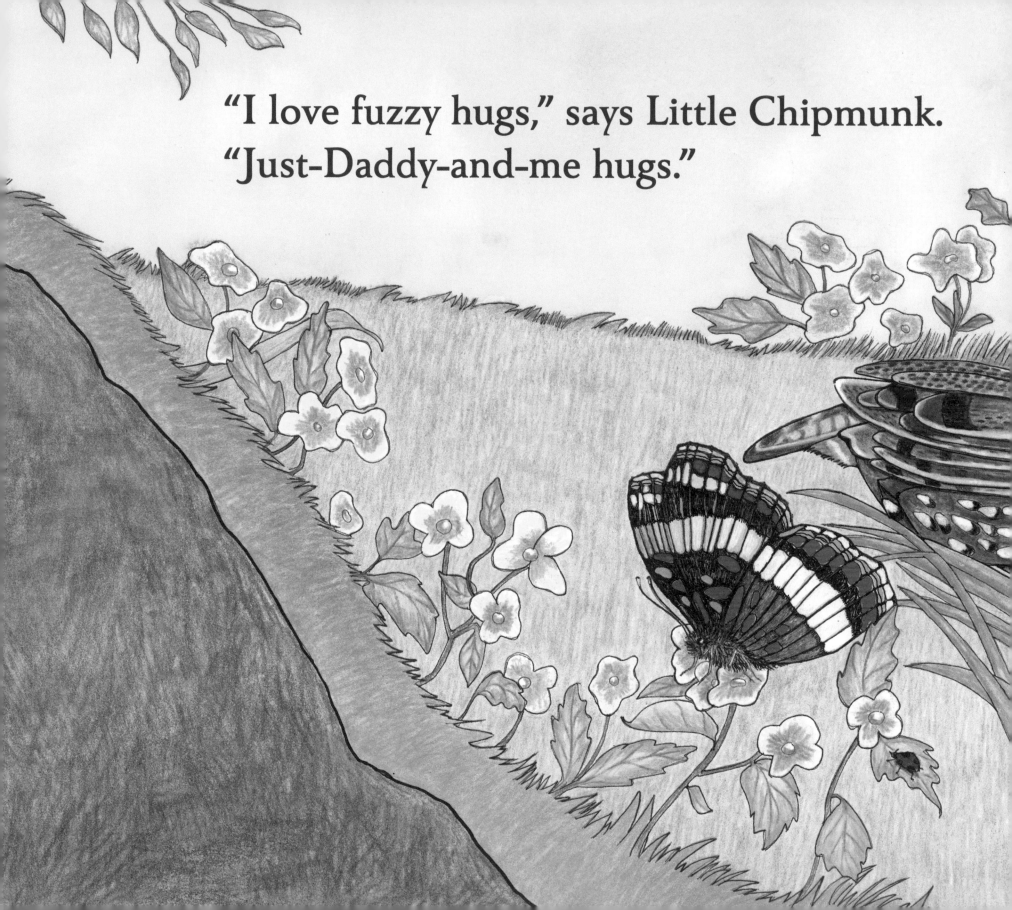

"I love feathered hugs," says Little Bobwhite.
"Just-Daddy-and-me hugs."

"I love silky hugs," says Little Hare.
"Just-Daddy-and-me hugs."

Sniffle-sniffle-sniff!

"I love downy hugs," says Little Woodpecker.
"Just-Daddy-and-me hugs."

"I love bristly hugs," says Little Squirrel. "Just-Daddy-and-me hugs."

Tatche-
tatche-cheee!

Hoo-hoo-hoot!

"I love winged hugs," says Little Owl.
"Just-Daddy-and-me hugs."

Urr-Urrr-Urrr!

There are all kinds of Daddy hugs,
but the best hug of all . . .

. . . is Daddy's hug good night.

Sweet dreams, my little one!

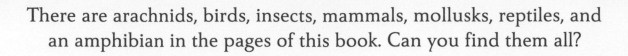

There are arachnids, birds, insects, mammals, mollusks, reptiles, and an amphibian in the pages of this book. Can you find them all?

PAGES 2–3
Raccoon (*Procyon lotor*)
Sawfly larva (*Craesus septentrionalis*)

PAGES 4–5
Painted turtle (*Chrysemys picta*)
White-lipped forest snail (*Triodopsis albolabris*)
Raccoon (*Procyon lotor*)

PAGES 6–7
Painted turtle (*Chrysemys picta*)
Dragonfly (Anisoptera)

PAGES 8–9
North American beaver (*Castor canadensis*)
Great spangled fritillary (*Speyeria cybele*)

PAGES 10–11
Striped skunk (*Mephitis mephitis*)
Spotted salamander (*Ambystoma maculatum*)
Honeybee (Apini)

PAGES 12–13
Black bear (*Ursus americanus*)
Boxelder bug (Genus *Leptocoris*)

PAGES 14–15
Red fox (*Vulpes vulpes*)
Broad-winged katydid (*Microcentrum rhombifolium*)

PAGES 16–17
Least chipmunk (*Eutamias minimus*)
Black carpenter ant (*Camponotus pennsylvanicus*)
White Admiral (*Limentitis arthemis*)

PAGES 18–19
Bobwhite (*Colinus virginianus*)
White-lipped forest snail (*Triodopsis albolabris*)

PAGES 20–21
Brown hare (*Lepus europaeus*)
Trichogramma wasp (Hymenoptera)

PAGES 22–23
Downy woodpecker (*Picoides pubescens*)
Orb weaver (Araneidae)

PAGES 24–25
Eastern gray squirrel (*Sciurus carolinensis*)
Red-humped appleworm (*Schizura concinna*)
Western meadowlark (*Sturnella neglecta*)

PAGES 26–27
Barn owl (*Tyto alba*)
Firefly (*Lampyridae*)

PAGES 28–29
Raccoon (*Procyon lotor*)
Eastern cottontail (*Sylvilagus floridanus*)

PAGES 30–31
Eastern cottontail (*Sylvilagus floridanus*)
Firefly (Lampyridae)

Ladybird beetles (Coccinellidae)
are pictured throughout.

ABOUT THIS BOOK

While working on *All Kinds of Kisses*, with its farm animals and sounds, the woodland animals around me began to audition . . . and that's when I started imagining the daddy hugs that they all might share!

The illustrations for this book were done in watercolor paints and pencil on Arches paper.
The text and display type are set in Carre Noir.

This book was edited by Liza Baker and designed by Saho Fujii with art direction from Patti Ann Harris.
The production was supervised by Erika Schwartz, and the production editor was Wendy Dopkin.

Copyright © 2014 by Nancy Tafuri • Jacket art © 2014 by Nancy Tafuri • Jacket design by Saho Fujii • Jacket copyright © 2014 Hachette Book Group, Inc. • All rights reserved. In accordance with the U.S. Copyright Act of 1976, the scanning, uploading, and electronic sharing of any part of this book without the permission of the publisher is unlawful piracy and theft of the author's intellectual property. If you would like to use material from the book (other than for review purposes), prior written permission must be obtained by contacting the publisher at permissions@hbgusa.com. Thank you for your support of the author's rights. • Little, Brown and Company • Hachette Book Group • 237 Park Avenue, New York, NY 10017 • Visit our website at lb-kids.com • Little, Brown and Company is a division of Hachette Book Group, Inc. The Little, Brown name and logo are trademarks of Hachette Book Group, Inc. • The publisher is not responsible for websites (or their content) that are not owned by the publisher. • First Edition: December 2014 • Library of Congress Cataloging-in-Publication Data • Tafuri, Nancy. • Daddy hugs / Nancy Tafuri. — First edition. • pages cm • Summary: Various young woodland animals describe, in their own unique ways, what they love most about hugs from their fathers. Includes a list of creatures hidden in the pictures for readers to find. • ISBN 978-0-316-22923-4 (hc) • [1. Hugging—Fiction. 2. Father and child—Fiction. 3. Forest animals—Fiction.] I. Title. • PZ7.T117Dad 2015 • [E]—dc23 • 2013044617 • 10 9 8 7 6 5 4 3 2 1 • SC • Printed in China